HELL HATH NO *Fury*

An Endless World Novella

An Endless World Novella

Visit Mandi Oyster online at
www.MandiOyster.com

Facebook: https://www.facebook.com/MandiOysterAuthor
Instagram: https://www.instagram.com/MandiOyster/

*For everyone who dared
to make their dreams come true.*

Trigger Warnings

*This book contains adult themes
and descriptions of death and grief.*

Reader discretion is advised.

Chapter 1

The Endless

Kit hovered above me in all of his glory. His skin was bare, his muscles taut. I blinked, trying to fully wake myself. We'd already celebrated our twentieth anniversary a few times, but Kit was an insatiable lover who brought out the best in me. Maybe it was because he was the first man I'd truly loved. The first man I'd ever been able to be myself with. My other half. Or maybe he was just that good.

Either way, I reached up to pull him back to bed. If he wanted more, who was I to say no? As my fingers neared his arm, a cloud shifted. The full moon's light shone through my bedroom window, glinting off the edge of his blade.

My hand stilled between us before falling to the mattress. A burning, aching lump formed in the back of my throat.

"I'm sorry, Ziah." Kit's voice cracked. "I can't watch him do it again."

Do it again? Do what? Those questions, along with a thousand others, raced through my mind when I realized what was happening, but the one that hurt the most was that after all of our years together, he didn't even have the decency to challenge me to a duel.

His betrayal felt like a punch to the gut, sickening me, but I stared up at him, holding his gaze as my fingers inched closer to my sword. If I was going to survive this, I had to silence my thoughts and turn off all my emotions except anger. That one I harnessed as if it was one of my horses. I knew it could be more volatile than a wild stallion, but I could control it. I would.

I let rage's blaze tear through me, fueling my motions, burning away the pain.

"You know the rules." He pinched his eyes closed, seeming to steel himself.

I didn't wait. I took the opportunity to wrap my hand around my sword's hilt.

"I will love you forever." Tears dripped down his cheeks, falling on my bare skin, and he positioned his sword over my heart, hesitating for only a moment before plunging it down. "Til the last one stands."

Death stared at me, and my life with Kit flashed through my mind.

Chapter 2

Memories

Twenty Years Earlier

My chest tightened as a familiar, if unexpected, pulse slammed into me, nearly dropping me to my knees. I braced one hand on the hood of my truck and the other on my chest while I scanned the area.

Few immortals stumbled into Laramie, and even fewer of them walked away. This was my territory, my domain, and though I didn't go searching for fights, I didn't back down when they came looking for me.

I reached inside my drover and grasped my sword. September in this part of Wyoming was too hot to be wearing a leather coat, but I needed somewhere to sheath my blade.

My gaze slid over the few people lingering outside of Safeway and came to a stop on the man staring back at me. He tipped his head and lifted his lips, revealing dimples beneath his dark scruff.

The tension eased from my body, and for some stupid reason, I found myself smiling back as I strode toward him. My boots thumped against the ground in a steady beat. The ever-present Laramie winds blew my long, brown hair over my shoulder and across my face. I brushed it back, pulling it out of my gray eyes, wishing I would have braided it before heading out that morning.

The man's hands were tucked in his jeans pockets with his thumbs sticking out. Casual. Relaxed. No weapon in sight. Still, I stopped more than an arm's length away. "I am Keziah Hale."

His eyes roved over me, stopping when they met mine. "So you're The Bear."

"Yeah." I sighed and shook my head. "Let me tell ya, it's not a pleasant way to die."

He lifted his hand to his mouth, but with dimples like his, it didn't hide the fact that he was smiling. "I don't think any of them are." He bowed slightly. "Kit Wallace."

Digging through my memories, I tried to remember any mention of him. I couldn't think of one time that his name had come up, though. "No, I don't imagine they are."

While he assessed me, I took in his measure. He stood at least six inches taller than me. That was a huge advantage for him in a fight, but I was shorter than most of the Endless I'd killed. Their height gave them a longer reach, but I was quick, agile, and more often than not, underestimated.

I looked into his whiskey-colored irises and wondered what lingered behind them. They sparkled with an inner light, making him look friendly, harmless, but I'd met too many monsters with honest eyes to believe they were windows to the soul. Too many evil spirits lingered behind kind eyes. "This isn't the place for a fight. We can take it to Pilot Hill or Bamforth. No one will see us there."

"I'm not looking for a fight." He lifted his hands in the air and nodded toward the store. "Just some groceries."

Then he did something no other Endless had ever done to me. He tucked his hands in his pockets, started whistling a jaunty melody, turned his back, and strode toward the grocery store with me trailing behind him, staring at the way his jeans hugged his butt and wondering if he was brave or stupid for not carrying a sword.I followed him through the doors and grabbed a shopping cart.

We headed in separate directions, but somehow he ended up in line right behind me. Dread skittered up my spine, and I turned so that I could keep an eye on him while I rang up my groceries. I'd only ever trusted one Endless with my life, and he'd died nearly a hundred years ago.

While I contemplated whether or not Kit would be dumb enough to attack me in public, he rubbed the back of his neck. "Can I make you dinner?"

I stared into his eyes and wondered if he had ulterior motives. Nothing malicious seemed to hide in their depths, but I'd been wrong before.

He shifted his weight, and I realized it was taking me far too long to answer him. "Maybe next time, Dimples." I paid for my groceries and waited for my receipt.

"Dimples, huh?" He grinned, and those dimples appeared again.

My heart stuttered at the sight, but I held firm.

He lifted the package of steaks before setting it on the conveyor belt. "You sure? I can grill with the best of them."

"I'm sure." I pushed my cart toward the doors. While I grabbed my bags out of it, he caught up to me and walked with me to the parking lot.

"Next time, then." He threw his groceries into the backseat of his navy crew cab, then climbed inside, and pulled onto the street.

Once his truck disappeared into the distance, I drove home.

The next time I went to Laramie, Dimples was standing in Safeway's parking lot. The tell-tale pulse of another Endless ripped through me. I considered turning around and going to one of the other grocery stores, but I didn't want him to think I was a coward.

Leaning against his truck, he loosed his smile on me when I parked next to him. As soon as I opened my door, he folded his hands behind him and rocked back on his heels. Once again, there was nowhere for him to hide a sword. "Dinner?"

"Persistent." An unexpected lightness filled my chest while butterflies fluttered in my stomach. I hopped out and felt my eyebrows pinch together as I surveyed my surroundings. Maybe twenty vehicles were in the lot, and the only person I saw out and about was Kit. "How'd you know I'd be here today?"

He closed the distance to me, moving cautiously, as if he expected me to hop back inside my truck and drive away at any moment. "I didn't. I've waited here every day since we met. I hoped you'd come back eventually."

Heat flooded through me, and my pulse ratcheted. How long had it been since someone had seen me as a woman? "It can't be that hard for you to get a date."

"It's a—" he rubbed his jaw, giving me the impression that he was searching for the right words "—bit difficult to find someone with shared life experiences." He lifted his hands, and one side of his mouth quirked up, revealing just a hint of his dimple. "And, I always feel like I'm robbing the cradle."

I laughed. "Yeah, there is that." Rolling my head from shoulder to shoulder, I debated what to do. He was right, though. No matter how many mortal men I met, I couldn't relate to them. "How about a late lunch instead? I have to get my groceries and get back in time to tend to my horses."

He smacked his hands together and beamed at me. His dimples sunk deeper into his cheeks than I'd seen before. "You driving, or am I?"

I didn't know this man well enough to climb inside his truck with him, so I opened my door and waved him over. As I drove down 3rd Street, the silence inside the cab pressed down on me. I clutched the steering wheel and glanced at him through the corner of my eye.

"Relax, Keziah." He chuckled under his breath. "You're acting like this is your first date."

I pulled into a parking spot along the street. "Call me Ziah." I tugged the key out of the ignition. "It's not my first date, but it's my first date this century."

"So you haven't dated in four years?" He opened his door and stepped onto the curb.

I shrugged. "Or forty. I hope the Crow Bar is okay." I nodded toward the restaurant that was attached to several other buildings.

"Whatever works for you." He stepped onto the sidewalk and waited for me.

I held the door open while he walked inside. It was a cozy place with paintings and chalkboards on the walls. In the winter, it tended to be a little chilly, but in September, it was comfortable. A lit-up crow with its wings spread watched over the restaurant from its corrugated metal perch above the kitchen. Kit's gaze roved over every detail while we waited to be seated.

We were led to a table in the back where we perused our menus in silence. When the waitress returned with our drinks, I ordered a Raven burger and beer-battered onion rings. Kit asked for the Crowburger and Pad Thai fries.

We watched our waitress stroll away, and once I knew she wouldn't be around for a while, I folded my arms on the table and leaned toward Kit. "How old are you?"

"Thirty-one." He grinned and took a drink of his Moose Drool.

I squeezed my eyes shut and shook my head. "Sorry." I pushed my chair back. "I can't date a younger man."

He reached across the table and settled his hand on mine. My first reaction was to jerk away, but warmth spread through my fingers, and I savored the contact.

His eyes sparkled when I relaxed. "I'm 179."

"Oh, that's so much worse." I slid my hand out from under his, picked up my silverware, and pulled the paper napkin ring off, rolling it up and then unrolling it. "I died when I was thirty-three. 180 years ago."

He wagged his eyebrows and growled playfully. "I always wanted to date a cougar."

With that out of the way, we steered the conversation toward subjects that could be overheard, and to my surprise, I found I was enjoying myself.

When I dropped him off at Safeway, he lifted my hand to his lips and pressed a kiss to the back of it, sending tingles racing up my arm. Butterflies fluttered against my stomach, and I felt as giddy as a schoolgirl.

A week later, Dimples and I hiked the Medicine Bow Peak Trail. Standing next to the summit marker at 12,018 feet above sea level, Kit lifted his hand, stopping short of touching my face. "May I?" His whiskey-colored eyes seemed to glow with an inner fire.

I nodded, and he cupped my cheek, gently rubbing his thumb over my skin. He held my gaze while he leaned down. His lips brushed over mine, and he started to back away. Heat pooled in my belly. It had been too long since I'd kissed a man, and I wasn't going to let it end so quickly. I wrapped my arms around his neck and pulled his mouth down on mine, parting his lips with my tongue.

After several more dates, I invited him to my house to go horseback riding with me. Soon after, we decided it was stupid for him to keep paying for a hotel room, and he moved in with me.

Every moment spent with Kit, every touch, every smile, every laugh ran through my mind on an unending loop. Riding horses, hiking, sword fighting, sparring, snowmobiling, and spending our nights wrapped in each other's arms. We'd hidden away from the game for twenty years. To be with him, I would have hidden from it forever.

Chapter 3

The Inheritance

Present Day

"*T*il the last one stands." His cutlass plunged toward my unprotected heart.

Hundreds of years of practice lent him the speed and grace few others possessed, but I was one of them. I jerked my sword up, laying it on top of my breasts. His blade slammed into mine, jarring him and pressing the sharp edges of mine into my skin.

Kit stumbled off balance, and the tip of his sword scored me from just below my heart to my hip. He stared at the blood pooling on my naked body. "Ziah." His grip on his cutlass and his taut muscles loosened.

He seemed distraught, but he was the one who had attacked me.

While I slept, nonetheless.

I would never be able to trust him again, never believe the sweet nothings he whispered in my ear.

His betrayal thickened the air between us, making it nearly impossible to breathe. My throat ached as I held back tears.

I reached beneath my pillow, pulled my dagger out, and while he stared at the blood he'd spilled, I thrust the blade through his perfectly sculpted pecs into his heart.

The heart I thought had belonged to me.

"Why?" I whispered.

His eyes widened, and his cutlass crashed against his nightstand as it fell to the floor.

This had to be a nightmare. He loved me. I loved him. Why would he do this? Why now? We'd spent the night celebrating our twentieth anniversary. He'd bought me flowers. Taken me to dinner. Made love to me like it was our first time.

But ...

He'd known.

I swallowed the lump in my throat. He'd known it was the last.

Kit reached for the knife embedded to the hilt in his chest, but it was too late. A river of blood ran down his sternum, outlining his abs.

Golden light erupted from the wound, filling my bedroom with the brightness of the sun. The scream that tore from me was feral. "Why?" The word sucked every ounce of air from my lungs. I breathed in, and the breath caught on my sob.

Before Kit entered my life, it had been decades since I'd let someone in, but he had wormed his way into my heart. It started with a smile that showed dimples peeking through his scruffy beard. His eyes had lit up, and for the first time since Triston found me, I felt like I could trust another of my kind.

With him at my side, I felt truly alive. Immortality was lonely. Watching everyone I knew die, time and time again, and knowing I would have to battle nearly every Endless I met wore on me.

But then Kit found me. I thought we'd stand together until the end. I thought we'd defy the game. I thought we'd have eternity.

How many times could I watch someone I loved die before I descended into madness?

Flecks of gold spun in the air, moving faster and faster. A whirlwind tearing Kit's body apart.

The vortex stretched to the ceiling, spreading across it when it could climb no higher.

I'd never killed someone I loved before, and even though I felt like my heart was being ripped out of my chest, I held his gaze until the end. Memorizing every fleck in his warm whiskey eyes. Knowing this would be the last time I saw him.

Light spiraled above him. Beautiful and terrible. It rattled the walls and tore pictures from their hangers. Tendrils reached for me, caressing my body like the hands of a lover. Like Kit had only hours before. Then all at once, the inheritance slammed into me with the force of a volcano erupting.

I screamed as Kit's power surged through my body like lava flowing through my veins.

My skin glowed from within, brightening as I arched off the bed and hovered above it.

The last of the golden embers pierced my body, filling me until I thought I would burst. Everything stilled as if the world held its breath. Then with a final surge, golden light blasted out of me. Shattering my windows and throwing me back down on the bed.

Every cell in my body ached, but nothing hurt as badly as the fragments of my broken heart.

Chapter 4

Consequences

Raindrops splashed on my face, jolting me awake. I stretched my hand across the bed, reaching for Kit, but he wasn't there.

The events from the previous night played through my mind, and my eyes sprang open. I clutched the sheets where he should have been and rolled over, burying my face in his pillow. It muffled my scream.

He'd never be there again.

"Oh, Kit." A sob caught in my throat, and I flopped onto my back, wrapping my arms around my body. "Why?"

As my heart shattered again, I took in the destruction that surrounded me.

Curtains and blinds hung haphazardly in front of windows that had exploded. Kit's sword pierced one of the logs that made up the walls, jutting out from it. The only decoration remaining hanging. Everything that adorned them before the inheritance ripped Kit apart littered the floor.

The bedroom was one of the only rooms in the house without wood floors. The carpet was a mix of tans and browns that concealed splintered pieces of wood and shards of glass. The clothes Kit and I wore on our date were strewn all about.

Hoping to avoid most of the debris, I climbed off the end of the bed. For the first time I could remember, I didn't bother to pull up the burgundy comforter. I snatched Kit's shirt off the floor and held it to my nose. His scent clung to the fabric. The smell was distinctly him. Almond and cedar with a hint of leather.

I stumbled to the shower and tried to wash away my memories. Instead, I thought of every time Kit had joined me beneath the spray, his toned body pressed against mine. I pictured his brown hair, turning nearly black and straightening beneath the stream. I saw the mischief in his eyes as he reached for the soap. I felt his hands as they washed my back and held me while water poured over us. I remembered his kisses trailing along my neck and down my arms. I'd fit perfectly in his embrace.

We'd been made for each other. The thought cut deeper than Kit's blade had. The sudden rush of grief staggered me, nearly dropping me to my knees.

"Why, Kit? Why'd you give up on us?" I remembered him kneeling on the bed, hovering above me, and wondered why he waited for the dead of the night.

The water washed away my tears, but the pain and regret remained.

When the stream became too cold to stand beneath, I turned the shower off and wrapped a towel around myself. Kit wasn't the first Endless who had betrayed me, but he was the only one I'd loved. The others danced through my memories. Friends. Acquaintances. One-night stands. They'd all taken a piece of me with them when they'd attacked. But Kit's death had shattered my heart. The shards stabbed my lungs, making it nearly impossible to breathe.

I clutched my chest and stared at my reflection in the mirror. The woman looking back at me had trusted too easily. Fallen too hard. "Never again."

I wiped the fog away. "I will never let someone get that close to me again. No more betrayals. No more heartache." Backing away, I dropped the towel and pulled my clothes on. "This stupid game isn't going to beat me. I'll harden my heart til the last one stands."

"What happened here?" The contractor stared into the bedroom. His broad frame took up most of the doorway. His Wyoming Cowboys hat covered most of his graying hair and shadowed his pale blue eyes.

Shrugging, I pinched my lips together and hoped to pull off some semblance of nonchalance. "My boyfriend and I were playing a game. I guess he didn't like losing." I waved my hand at the window. I'd picked up most of the mess, but it still resembled the battle scene it was.

The man seemed to grow, standing taller and puffing his chest out. "I've got some guys. We can take care of him."

"I'm not worried about him." Not wanting to break down in front of a total stranger, I took several deep breaths. "I won't be seeing him again."

He settled his hand on my shoulder, the gesture both protective and comforting. "If he comes around, you let me know."

Once the contractor left, the silence of the house closed in on me. I strapped on my sword and walked to the barn. The Little Laramie River rushed by on the side of my property. Trees grew all along the water, and I could just glimpse Snowy Range from my house.

After my rebirth, I fled to Wyoming and eventually settled near what would become Centennial. Since I didn't age, I had to leave from time to time, returning after most people who knew me had passed. I sucked in a breath of fresh mountain air and realized I'd probably been here too long already. Twenty-five years had passed in a flash, and I hadn't aged at all.

With that thought adding to the weight on my shoulders, I opened the barn door to the nickers of horses. Ripley, my blue roan, stuck his head over the stall door, and I rubbed my hand along his blaze. He lipped my shoulder, pulling me closer. I fell into him, wrapping my arms around his neck, and sobbed into his fur.

I cried until I had no more tears. The love of my life was dead at my hands. I would never know why he'd turned on me, but I had to accept his death and move on. There was no other way.

I grabbed a brush. With each stroke, I felt a little more at peace. Once Ripley's fur shone, I ran my hand down his leg, lifting it and setting his hoof on my thigh. I grabbed the pick and cleaned the dirt and debris around his shoe. After scraping each hoof, I hugged him again, then let him out into the barnyard.

Breathing deeply, I walked to Amala's stall and stared at the paint who'd taken to Kit from the very first time he'd gone riding with me. Knowing she would sense any negativity, I focused on the good times while I brushed her.

Twenty Years Earlier

Kit and I raced across my property. The thunder of the horses' hooves was music to my ears. We brought them to a stop at the creek and let them drink. Then we rode to a clearing where Kit laid a blanket on the ground, and I sat out our picnic.

"You know, I was just passing through Laramie." He poured a glass of wine for each of us. "I never expected to find you." He grabbed my hand and pulled me down on top of him, catching me as easily as a grizzly catches a spawning salmon.

I giggled as I snuggled against him. "Well, I'm glad fate stepped in." I pressed a kiss to his neck, and when he sucked in a breath, I trailed kisses along his jaw until he grabbed my face and crashed his mouth down on mine.

While the horses grazed and the food remained untouched, Kit slid his hands under my shirt. His fingers skimmed along my sides, raising goosebumps and heating my core. He slipped his hands into my sleeves, a silent question.

I lifted my arms, and he tugged my shirt over my head. With the mountains watching, we made love for the first time.

Present Day

I stroked Amala's muzzle. "He's gone, sweetie." I opened the stall door and let her out into the barnyard with Ripley.

Chapter 5

Followed

For the next two days, I wallowed in self-pity, only getting out of the bed in the spare room to feed the horses. It would be at least a week before they began work on my room, and once it was done, I didn't know if I'd ever sleep in there again. Kit's ghost would forever haunt me. Any time I woke up in the middle of the night I would see him standing over me, see my blade pierce his heart, see the look in his eyes as he was torn apart by the inheritance.

On the third day, I dragged myself out of bed and took a shower. It was time for me to pull myself together. I had to go to Laramie for groceries. Ripley and Amala needed carrots and oats.

My heart sank when I stepped into the garage. Kit's truck was parked next to mine. The navy paint was spotless. The silver shone even in the dim light of the enclosed space. I climbed into my truck and slammed it into reverse, trying not to look at his as I backed out, but my gaze was drawn to it. I saw him sitting behind the wheel. He grinned at me, and his dimples sunk deep into his cheeks.

I stomped on the gas pedal and pushed the button to shut the garage door before the front of my truck was even out of the way. How long would I see Kit's ghost? How long would he haunt me?

I blared the radio, playing upbeat music that I hoped would keep my thoughts from drifting. Between Centennial and Laramie were vast open areas. Pronghorn dotted the fields, and crows sat on fence poles. White bubbly clouds hovered against the cyan sky that seemed so much closer than anywhere else I'd been. The miles of open country stretched on with too much room for me to think.

My hand ached to hold Kit's as I'd done on nearly every trip for the past twenty years. I tightened my grip on the wheel and tried to ignore the tingling in my palm and fingers.

Once I reached Laramie, Kit was everywhere I went. The parking lot, the store, the drive home. He watched me. His eyes filled with accusations.

I slowed down to pull into my driveway, and instead of passing me, the car behind me stayed there. It crept by when I stopped at the mailbox. I didn't recognize the vehicle and couldn't catch a glimpse of the driver. Even though I didn't feel an Endless, a niggling feeling of danger crept up my spine.

My log cabin-style house sat back from the road, nestled up against the trees, but visible enough from the road. A buck and rail fence separated my property from the road. The porch that wrapped all of the way around the house made it look homey. That and the stone chimney that climbed up the side and extended beyond the roof were my favorite things. I loved sitting by a cozy fire, watching the snow fall while I devoured a good book.

As soon as I pulled into the garage, I closed the door. I had to squeeze behind the truck to get in the house, but it was better than worrying about whether or not I was still being watched. I entered through the mudroom, left the overhead lights off, and let my eyes adjust before putting the groceries away in the kitchen.

I ducked down and crept like a common thief to the living room window. Squatting, I peeked through the blinds. The car was still parked on the side of the road just past my driveway.

I rocked back on my heels. Why would someone be following me? Nobody could know what happened to Kit. He didn't have any family, and in the twenty years we'd been together, nobody had come looking for him. The life of an immortal was a lonely one.

Staying low, I scrambled back to the mudroom, grabbed a gun, strapped on my sword, and hurried down the stairs to the basement. There were tunnels from the house to the barn so the horses could be tended in the winter. I ran through the underground passage. Lights hung on the cement walls, guiding my way. There was only one entrance and one exit. Steps led to a hatch. I opened it, and the soothing scent of horses hit me. Earthy and musky with just a hint of sweetness. I stepped out and closed the trapdoor as carefully as possible. As I walked by, Ripley and Amala greeted me. I patted each of them on the neck, hoping that whoever was out there didn't hear them, then snuck out the back door.

Sticking to the shadows, I made my way to the road where I waited for clouds to cover the moon before darting across. Then I watched. The driver faced my house, holding binoculars to his eyes. He looked to be about twenty-five, and I couldn't remember ever seeing him before.

I glanced toward my house, wondering if he was watching something other than me. Moose and elk frequented my property, and occasionally, a black bear would wander through my yard. Narrowing my eyes, I searched for anything that might have caught his attention, but there was nothing.

I returned my focus to the driver. His vigil was unwavering. After another fifteen minutes or so, it must've gotten stuffy in his car because he rolled the window down.

I waited while he settled back into his watch. Then I crept to the car. Like a rattler striking, I reached up and wrapped my hand around his neck. "What are you doing here?" Anger coiled inside of me, deepening my voice.

Chapter 6

Chroniclers

"I-I thought ..." He trembled in my grasp. "I-I thought I saw a bear."

My fingers tightened. "So you've been waiting for it to return for nearly an hour?" In the two hundred thirty-three years I'd been alive, I couldn't remember wanting to punch another human being so badly. "I'll give you a second to come up with a better story."

"I—"

"Time's up." I reached in with my other hand and snatched the keys out of the ignition. "Who sent you?"

He tried to turn his head, but I didn't loosen my grip. "Nobody sent me."

"Then what do you want with me?" I flicked his ear. "The only thing out here to look at is me. There are no other houses. Nobody else."

He cowered but couldn't pull away. "I was staking your place out. You're out here in the middle of nowhere, with no one watching. His eyes darted from side to side, never meeting mine. I was planning on robbing you."

"What a dumbass." I slammed my hand down on his door frame. "Wanna try again?"

He whimpered. "I-I'm a Peeping Tom, okay!"

"My patience is wearing thin." I loosened my grip enough for him to turn toward me. Real fear widened his pupils, making the green of his irises just a thin ring. "And it's really easy to hide a body out here."

A whiff of rank body odor filled my nostrils. The man's gaze slid to mine and then away. "Where's Kit?" He glanced at me again, and that time, I saw genuine concern in his eyes. "I haven't seen him for three days."

"Kit's gone." My hand dropped along with my stomach. The pain clawed at my heart.

His gaze turned vacant, and his mouth floundered. "Gone? Like left? Or gone? Like gone? Final death gone?"

I staggered back. "Final death gone. What's that supposed to mean?"

"You know what I mean, Keziah." He smacked his hands down on the steering wheel. "I know what you are. I know what he was." He dragged his fingers through his hair. "It was my job to watch him."

Every word out of his mouth tore through me. "What do you mean it was your job?"

His eyes widened. "I can't talk to you about this. Please, just forget I was here."

"Seriously?" I stood straighter and folded my arms over my chest. "You can talk, or I can call the cops and tell them you've been stalking me."

He dragged his hand through his hair, and I envied him when it laid down perfectly. "You were never supposed to know about me."

"Well, I do." I flipped my hands up. "Spill. Now."

He leaned back against the headrest. "I am a Chronicler. There is one of us for each of you. We record your histories. Kit was the subject of my book. Most of the world would think it was a fantasy novel, but it was his life." He slumped forward, holding his head in his hands. "I never met him, but somehow … he felt like my closest friend."

I stood outside his car and stared up at the sky. Along with the moon, millions of stars dotted the velvety black canvas. I inhaled slowly and released each breath even slower.

"Who killed him?" The man sounded nearly as broken as I felt.

I saw Kit standing above me. Naked as a newborn babe. Then his sword plunged toward my heart. I pressed my hand to my chest, covering the ache. "I did."

"You … no." Jerking his head back, he gasped. His mouth hung open, and he looked like he was searching for the words. "Why? You loved him. I know you did. I saw you together."

I rubbed my chest, fighting the tightness, struggling to suck in a breath. "He was—" I choked on a sob "—my world." I turned around and slid down the car until I was sitting on the ground. "It was self-defense."

A male fox's scream tore the still night, reminding me of the tortured sound my soul made when I killed Kit.

There was no response from the man in the car. The silence pressed down on me, threatening to bury me beneath the guilt. "Who watches me?"

As soon as the words were out of my mouth, another more pressing question took its place. "What do they watch me do?"

"We watch everything. We document it." His voice rose. "It's amazing. All the things you've seen. All the things you've done. All the things you've lived through. The way you take each change in stride and continuously adapt."

Change … Had Kit changed so much that my death would mean nothing to him? "Why would he do it?" I pulled my knees up and bent over them, curling in on myself, hoping to ease the pain. "He loved me, didn't he?"

He opened his door, got out, and sat next to me on the ground. "He loved you."

It was what I wanted to hear, but it made no sense. "Why'd he do it then?"

"Why don't you read my book?" He stood and reached his hand down to me. "You can fill in some gaps for me and maybe find some answers."

Cocking my head to the side, I stared at him for several seconds. "Why the sudden change? Why do you want to help me?"

"I know this sounds stupid, but Kit was—" he swallowed hard, and his eyes misted over "—almost like a brother to me. I knew everything about him, and now he's gone."

I slid my hand into his and allowed him to pull me up. "You have me at a disadvantage. You know my name, but I don't know yours."

"Noah. Noah Greymark."

I met Noah at The Library Sports Grille & Brewery in Laramie. This particular library was a bar and restaurant. Bookshelves lined the walls, and TVs showed whatever games were playing. Jerseys hung between the screens, and Steamboat, Wyoming's bucking horse with his rider, was painted on the gold wall.

Noah sat across the table from me and slid a binder over the wooden surface. "It's not the final draft. There are probably a ton of mistakes, but it's a start."

I rubbed my hand over the cover. The idea of opening it made me nauseous. But I wanted to know. "You're not that old." I shot him what I hoped was a smile. "So how far back can this go?"

"All the way before his first death." He pulled the wrapper off his straw and shoved it into his glass. "There are records from that far back. I used them for everything up until seven years ago."

I watched him. "What made you become a ..." I tipped my head to the side, trying to remember what he'd said. "What was it?"

"Chronicler." He held his straw to the side and drank straight out of the glass. "I was in a wreck. Buddy o' mine was driving. He died, and I was trapped. The car caught on fire, and I knew I was a goner, but he woke up and pulled me out before ..." He rolled his sleeve up and showed me his arm. Scars climbed from his wrist to his shoulder, and I imagined the flames doing the same. "It was bad, but it could've been so much worse. I still have my pretty face."

His words drew my gaze to his face. Even though he looked young, I could see the torment that hid behind his green eyes. His dark blond hair was medium-length, and he kept pushing his bangs back. He had a strong chin, and I had to admit, a handsome face.

"I'm glad you got out." I looked back down at the book he'd passed to me. "What happened to your friend?"

"He walked away, pretended nothing had happened." Suddenly, his eyes seemed to glisten a little more. "From what I heard, an Endless killed him before he knew what he was."

The waitress brought our food over. I picked at my fries, and Noah didn't eat much more. The weight of our conversation stifled any hunger we might have had.

"One of the Chroniclers found me in the hospital and gave me a choice." He stared at something behind me, but since my back was to the wall, I wasn't concerned. I figured all he saw were his memories. "I had to know more … if it would happen to me."

"And …" My pulse raced. The idea that we could know in advance … That someone could be there for us when we died … Instead of facing the world lost and alone, confused about what was happening.

But then again, there were those who would wait for an Endless to be born and then kill them immediately.

Trying not to let on how interested I was, I picked up my burger and held it in front of my mouth. "Have they found a way to tell?"

He shook his head, then brushed his bangs out of his eyes. "Apparently, there are some Endless who can sense others who've yet to turn, but they're rare."

"Hopefully, they're the honorable ones."

"Not all of them." He suddenly sounded much older than he appeared—like the weight of the world had already dragged him down. "That's never the way the world works."

I set my burger on my plate and wiped my fingers on my napkin. "No, it never is. Is it?"

Chapter 7

Truth is Stranger Than Fiction

Kit's book sat on the passenger seat. For the forty-minute drive home, my gaze kept getting pulled to it. The story of his life, at least everything they'd watched him do, was written in those pages. It wasn't the beginning that concerned me, though. I wanted to know what could have changed him, what could have made him want to kill me.

Would I find what I was looking for inside, or would it just leave me with more questions?

When I got home, I set the book on the table and ran my fingers over the black binder. I started to open it, but my hand shook. I jerked it back, clutching my fist in my other hand, trying to stop the trembling. All the while, I stared down at the book.

I had no business reading his story. I'd ended him. I could have let him live. I could have sent him away. He wouldn't be mine, but he'd be alive.

My hand trailed my body where Kit's sword had scored my skin. I should have a scar, something to show for that night, for all our years together and how they'd ended, but when I'd woken the next morning, my skin had looked as flawless as it had before the bear attacked me. No marks from that fateful day stayed on my skin, and none had since. My limbs grew back. My skin stitched itself together. The only way death could find me was if my heart was damaged beyond repair.

Despite the way it felt, my continued existence proved my heart was still intact.

I turned my back on the book and walked into the kitchen. While I chopped vegetables and diced chicken, my gaze was pulled to the binder sitting on the table. The thought of opening it made me nauseous, and the thought of leaving it unread was even worse.

I put a pat of butter in a frying pan, then added the chicken and vegetables to it. I dumped rice into a pot of boiling water, covered it, and pulled it off the heat. While the chicken sizzled, I walked to the table.

My fingers skimmed over the cover, and this time, I managed to open it.

Kit stared up at me from the first page. I couldn't pull my gaze away from his beautiful whiskey-colored eyes. My breath caught as I remembered the last time I'd seen them. I tried to release it, but it lodged in my throat.

The acrid smell of burning food pulled me back into the present. As I stepped away, I noticed what was under the photo: Kit Wallace 1825-2024.

One hundred ninety-nine years.

I stumbled back to the stove and stirred the chicken and vegetables. Kit had graced this planet with his presence for one hundred ninety-nine years, and I'd ended his life with one thrust of a blade.

I plated my dinner and walked to the table. I hadn't been able to eat lunch, and the thought of taking a bite of my supper turned my stomach.

Sitting at the table with my chicken and rice in front of me, I reached for the binder and flipped the pages toward the end of the book. If Noah had witnessed anything that had changed Kit's mind, it would have to be there. I ran my finger along the page and flipped to the next until I found a promising passage.

Downtown Laramie was bustling. Kit pulled his navy Silverado into a parking spot, and Noah couldn't believe his luck when a vehicle two spots down from it backed out. Noah sat in his car and watched Kit stride into 3rd Street Bar through his mirror.

As soon as the door closed, Noah followed. Sunlight streamed in through windows that made up most of the front of the bar. Once his eyes adjusted, he noticed Kit sitting in one of the wooden booths. The table behind him was empty, and Noah was grateful that luck seemed to be on his side. As Noah walked to it, Kit glanced around the way an Endless does when another one comes in proximity. Noah stood at the end of the table and took his time removing his jacket, looking around like he'd never been there before as he did. Giving him the perfect opportunity to watch the stranger enter.

The man stood out with his expensive suit and fancy cane. He strode forward like he not only owned the bar but also the entire city. He screamed power and money, not the type of man who frequented small bars in college towns. His black hair and beard were neatly trimmed. A diamond and gold earring stood out against his dark skin. He joined Kit, sliding into the booth and lifting his lip as if disgusted.

"Braunwin." Kit nodded at the man.

He folded his hands over his chest. "Just Braun these days." His brown eyes met Noah's, and Noah tossed his jacket onto the seat before sliding into the booth. With his back to Kit's, he sat his phone on the table and hit the record button.

Their words were hushed, but one of the reasons Noah made a good Chronicler was his ability to hyper-focus and tune out the rest of the world.

"Why is the Bear not dead?" There was accusation in Braun's voice.

A gasp tore from me. This was what I'd been looking for, but to actually see it there in front of me ... I guess I hadn't expected it. I read the sentence two more times. Had this really happened? Had Noah witnessed this interaction? And why did this Braun guy want me dead? Was that even his name?

I shoveled a bite of my food into my mouth while I contemplated what I'd read to this point.

There was some shuffling before Kit said, "I love her. From the moment I laid eyes on her, I've loved her."

"We had an accord." This was not a man who knew what it was to love. This was a man hardened by whatever life had thrown his way.

"Please." Emotion clogged Kit's voice. "Let me have her. Don't make me do this."

Another pause. "If you would have ended her twenty years ago like you were supposed to, you wouldn't have fallen so deeply. Maybe you've forgotten, but I own you. If she isn't dead by the end of the week, both of you will be."

Chapter 8

A Plan

$\mathcal{I}$n the twenty years we'd been together, Kit hadn't talked much about his first death. All I knew was that he had been shot and killed in one of the last battles in the Crimean War. He'd woken to find his troop decimated, so I understood his reluctance to discuss it. It had to have been horrible to see his friends and allies strewn about like broken toy soldiers, but when I asked who had found him, he'd brushed it off saying the man wasn't around anymore. I thought by gone, he meant dead. I should have pressed.

I ran my finger over the type, reading it again. A dull, hollow ache filled my chest. If somebody had given me the choice of killing Kit or being killed, I would've run my sword through that person's heart. I wouldn't have gone on a date with Kit, given him gifts, made love to him, and held him as he drifted off to sleep, all the while knowing I intended to kill him while he slept.

I pushed my plate away and grabbed my phone.

"Keziah, what's up?" Noah sounded as nervous as he had when I first approached him in his car.

I glanced over at the book, trying to figure out exactly what I wanted to say. "Hey, Noah. Please call me Ziah."

"Yeah, sure, I forgot."

I sucked in a deep breath, then released it slowly. "Do you know who Braun is?"

"I can't talk about him." He sounded regretful. "It's against my oath."

I rubbed my forehead with the hand that wasn't holding the phone. "Can you wait until I find him to ... to report Kit's death?"

"I wanted to talk to you about that." He paused for long enough that I wondered if I should break the silence, but I waited. "I was hoping you would tell me how it happened."

His words hit me like a punch in the gut. I sucked in a breath and held it while pain tore through me.

"Ziah, hello, Ziah? Are you there?"

The book sat next to me, and I imagined it ending with me stabbing Kit. What would the readers think when he attacked me? What would they think when I ended him? "I—" I wanted to tell him that I couldn't talk to him about it, but maybe I could use it as leverage instead. "If you wait until I find Braun, I'll ... I'll tell you what happened."

"I know it won't be easy for you." His voice turned compassionate. "It's not going to be easy for me to write it either. He was my first assignment. I should've been there when he died."

Anger flared up inside of me, burning away the pain and heartache. "Yeah, but you thought he would walk away, and I would be dead. How can you sleep at night knowing that you could have saved his life by saving mine?"

"I'm sorry, Ziah, but we can't."

I wished I could see his face, to know what he was thinking and how he really felt. "Why? Why can't you?"

"We can't take sides." There was a noise that sounded like he stood up, and if I had to guess, I would say he was pacing. "The Endless ... you kill to survive. We record your histories, but we don't get involved."

"Maybe you should." I carried my plate to the trash can and scraped my food off. "If one of the bad guys wins, the world will go to Hell. Worse than it's ever been." I rinsed the plate. "This Braun doesn't sound like a good guy. Let me find him before anyone else finds out about Kit. Let me end him."

Noah sighed. "I'm not sure if your Chronicler was there. I don't know what he knows or what he's reported." There was another long pause. "How are you going to find him?"

"Without your help, I'll have to go to Laramie, drive down every road, and hope to feel his presence. Once I find him, I'll end him."

Chapter 9

Mentor

Sleep brought with it an onslaught of nightmares, watching Kit's death over and over again without being able to rouse myself.

The sun shone between the slit in the curtains, shining on my eyes, and pulling me from the dream's hold. I sat up and held my face in my hands. My chest ached with Kit's loss. I felt like I'd been gutted and the hollowness inside would swallow me whole.

I went through the motions of my morning routine, getting dressed in my work clothes, tending to the horses, showering, and dressing again. I grabbed Kit's cowboy hat off the hook by the front door and threw on his coat, tucking my hair inside of it and pulling the collar up to block the lower half of my face. His smell clung to his drover. The mix of almond, cedar, and leather nearly dropped me to my knees. I braced my hand on the wall and waited for the scent to dissipate before grabbing his keys and striding into the garage.

If I thought wearing his hat and coat was bad, that had nothing on sitting behind the wheel of his truck. There his fragrance saturated the small, enclosed space. Even though there was a bite in the air, I rolled his window down as I backed out of the garage.

My Silverado had always been used for work, running into Laramie to pick up feed for the horses, fencing, and whatever else I'd needed for them. Kit's truck was the one we'd taken on our last date, and the memories slammed into me as I drove east on Snowy Range Road.

He'd turned up the radio and belted out some of my favorite songs along with me. Lifting our joined hands, he kissed the back of mine. "Twenty years, Ziah." He squeezed my fingers. "And eternity to come."

I pulled onto the shoulder and pushed the button for the hazard lights. How could he have said that? How could he have pretended when he'd known he was going to kill me later that night?

Despair washed over me, threatening to drown me beneath its waves, but I grabbed onto a lifeboat and dragged myself up. Staring into the distance, I wiped the tears from my face and pulled myself together. I could either be this sad pathetic creature, or I could find out why Kit turned against me.

Anger simmered in my chest. I let it burn through me until the rage consumed me, and I could only focus on one word, one name.

Braun.

I was the embodiment of the saying, "Hell hath no fury like a woman scorned."

I would end Braun if it was the last thing I did.

I pulled into the Shell gas station at the end of Snowy Range Road, then looked up 'hotels near me' on my phone. From Braun's description in Noah's book, I didn't take him for a camper, so I figured my best bet for finding him was to drive by each of the sixty-eight hotels. If I didn't find him at any of them, I'd have to expand my search to bed and breakfasts, Airbnbs, and everywhere else people rented out these days. Once I found him, I'd make him beg for his life.

I drove down Grand Avenue, then cruised all the back roads. I kept expecting to feel the pulse of another Endless, but the hours passed by without even a tingle. When I passed by the 3rd Street Bar, I pulled into a spot along the road and called Noah.

"Hey, Noah." I slumped back in the seat, pulling the cowboy hat low over my eyes as I did. "I read the book, and I'm looking for Braun."

There was a long pause on the other end. "I don't know where he's staying, and I couldn't tell you if I did."

"Did you happen to see what he drives? Or hear anything that might help me track him down?"

"Sorry." He sighed long and deep, and I knew I was wearing out my welcome. "I got there before him, and I stuck around for quite a while after they left. The last thing I wanted was for them to figure out that I was surveilling them."

"Yeah, I can't imagine that would have ended well ... with Braun anyway."

There was silence on the other end of the line. "I wish I could be more help, but I have to tread carefully here." I'd seen Noah run the gamut of emotions, so I knew he was being sincere. "I made an oath."

This was life and death, and he was worried about a damned oath. I shook my head and hoped not to sound too frustrated. "If you think of anything that helps, let me know."

"Good luck, Ziah. I hope you find the bastard and end him."

I hung up and pounded on the steering wheel. Eight billion people lived on the planet. How was I supposed to find one? I'd never been like some of the other Endless. I didn't hunt others to kill them. I minded my business and only killed when I had to. Even though I'd been alive for 233 years, this was new to me.

For the next three days, I donned Kit's hat and coat, went to the garage, and climbed behind the wheel of his truck. By the third day, his scent no longer slammed against me when I opened the door. I kept the windows rolled up, praying I could keep his fragrance contained for as long as possible.

I drove along the streets of Laramie, hoping to happen upon Braun. In a lot of other towns, I would be able to focus on the license plates, looking for one that stood apart from the others, but this was a college town with students from all over the country and from Canada. It was useless trying to find a vehicle that didn't belong.

After not finding Braun on the fourth day of searching, I drove home, changed into workout gear, grabbed my sword, and went outside. For the last twenty years, I'd sparred with Kit, but without him, I practiced kata, slowly moving, using my body as resistance, making sure each cut was perfect.

Focusing on the exercise cleared my mind. I hadn't given up on finding Braun, but I couldn't let him be my sole priority. I needed to be ready when I found him. I needed to avenge Kit and end the bastard who had destroyed my peace.

The old motions came back to me. Muscle memory from years of practicing. The movements reminded me of the Endless who'd taken pity on me.

Two Hundred Years Earlier

I rode my horse, Strudel, through a small fur traders' settlement. My hat was pulled low, my face was dirty, and my coat covered my body. All with the hope that nobody here would notice I was a woman on my own.

A pulse had slammed into me, nearly knocking me out of the saddle. It rang through my body, vibrating and growing louder. I clutched my head with one hand until the noise finally, thankfully trailed off.

Shaking off the strange sensation, I tugged on the reins and looked around, hoping to figure out what was happening. The feeling had never occurred before the grizzly attack, but that had been the second time in as many months that I'd felt it.

My gaze raked over all of the faces until I found one staring back at me.

The man pulled his drover to the side, exposing his gun. His eyes narrowed to slits as he strode toward me. His brown, bushy beard hid the majority of his face.

With each step he took, an impending sense of doom grew within me. "Did you feel that? Do you know what it is?"

"You're new." He patted Strudel's neck, and the Bay leaned into his touch.

I looked around. Wooden buildings lined both sides of the dusty street. "I have never been here before."

"No, that feeling." He wrapped my horse's reins around his wrist. "You died recently."

"I thought I did—" I rubbed my chest "—but here I am."

He led Strudel toward the rushing mountain stream. Water crashed over rocks. The sound, even though loud, was soothing to me. "You died." He pulled his arm out of his sleeve, grabbed a dagger, and slashed through his flesh.

"What are you doing?" My heart raced, and I couldn't tear my eyes away from the pooling blood. Why had he done that? If he would do that to himself, what would he do to me? Had he not held Strudel's reins, I would've galloped off and never looked back.

Instead, I stared at the wound, and my eyes widened when gold light flickered over the cut. Beneath the halo of energy, his skin stitched itself back together. "What the hell?" A sour taste filled my mouth, and I jerked away from him, falling off Strudel. I lay on the ground, staring up at the blue sky, trying to suck in a breath.

The man walked toward me, keeping one hand on Strudel the whole time. He reached down, grabbed my hand, and pulled me to my feet. "We are immortal. That feeling … it happens when another of us is near. Til the last one stands."

"Til the last one stands?" I pressed my hand to my chest and leaned forward. "What's that supposed to mean?"

He laughed, a sound that lacked all humor, instead filling me with dread. "Well, little lady, it's no life for a woman." His head bobbed up and down several times. "That's for sure. It means you need to learn how to kill or be killed."

I backed away from him, but he grabbed my arm. His blue gaze softened when I tensed. "I won't harm you, but others will if you don't guard your heart." He kept hold of me, leading me back toward the town. "Name's Triston."

"Keziah." I grabbed Studel's reins when we walked by her, and she followed along behind us. My thoughts kept circling back to "kill or be killed." I watched the man through the corner of my eyes, wondering if he would attack me. "Why didn't you kill me?"

Dust kicked up under our feet with each step we took. "I don't kill without reason, even for the game. I kill when challenged or when wronged. Good people don't deserve to die before they have a chance to shine their light on the world." He nodded toward a hitching post, and I tied Strudel's reins on it. "Help when you can, and hunt when you have to."

Triston took me under his wing, teaching me everything he knew about the game, about self-defense, and about living as an immortal. He'd been there when I'd made my first kill and held me through the night while I'd cried.

Present Day

I longed for Triston's guidance, his steady, comforting presence. If he were here now, he would tell me not to give up until I was serving Braun his own heart on a platter.

Chapter 10

Messages

Kit's phone was in my hand. The cord stretched over the carpet to the outlet on the wall. While I waited for his battery to charge, I sat on the couch with a warm fire crackling in the hearth and stared at nothing.

He'd tried to kill me. There couldn't be anything worse than that on his phone, but my gut churned at the thought of what I might find. I finished my glass of wine in a single gulp, then punched his password into his cell.

His background image was of me and him. We stood in front of Lake Marie and the Diamond.

The mountain reflected in the clear water, but I couldn't tear my eyes from him. The way he'd been looking at me when the picture was taken. There was so much love in his gaze. Why wouldn't he fight Braun instead of me? What kind of hold did that man have on him?

His text message app had the number 56 above it, so I decided to start there. The majority of the texts were from Braun Abara. No image. That would have been helpful, but at least, I had a last name for him. I clicked on his name and scrolled to the first unread message.

September 18:

Did you do it?

I saw you with her.

Zipping her dress.

A woman in love.

Did you look her in the eyes?

How did it feel?

Is it done?

Something came up, and I couldn't be there to witness the inheritance.

You know you had to do it.

Til the last one stands.

September 19:

Kit?

Should I be worried about you?

She didn't best you, did she?

I know this one was hard for you, but you need to respond.

September 20:

Maybe I should have done it myself.

You still owe me, though.

I could've ended your immortal life on that battlefield. Instead, I taught you everything you know.

September 21:

Why aren't you answering?

She better be gone.

September 22:

Meet me at 3rd Street Bar. 2:00.

I looked up from the phone, staring at the flames dancing in the fireplace, thinking back. I'd been at The Library that day, meeting Noah. If I'd thought of this earlier, I could have confronted him already. I could have killed him and gotten some closure. This could all be over, but it hadn't even occurred to me to look at Kit's phone until going through kata this afternoon. The physical activity seemed to recharge my brain.

I reached for my wine and frowned when I found the glass empty. I contemplated refilling it, but I'd left the bottle on the kitchen counter. Wiping my hand over my mouth, I turned back to the texts instead.

Don't be late.

You didn't show.

Should I be worried?

September 23:

Come on, Kit. I've seen you driving around Laramie.

I saved you.

I taught you everything.

This is how you repay me?

I know you did it.

Answer me!

September 24:

You're really starting to piss me off.

Answer your damn phone.

September 25:

Okay.

I get it.

You're grieving.

I won't bother you for a couple days.

But remember, if you don't answer me, you'll never be able to quit looking over your shoulder.

Don't forget.

You are mine.

The last message came in the night before, so if Braun was a man of his word, that gave me one more day before he came looking for Kit.

I held my thumbs over the keypad, trying to decide how to respond, finally settling on, "I'll be ready." I looked at the words for a few seconds before hitting send.

The bastard had played Kit like a fiddle, but I still didn't understand why Kit hadn't confided in me. Why he hadn't faced Braun or told me so I could.

"Aaagh!" I tossed his phone on the floor and rubbed my palm over my aching chest, hoping to dull the pain. "If I could just go back."

If only … Instead of plunging my dagger through his heart, we could have talked. We could have figured out a better way.

But armed with this knowledge, I would do everything in my power to end Braun.

Standing alongside the windows, I closed the blinds, shutting out the night. Knowing that Braun had been watching us sent shivers of dread racing up my spine.

The master bedroom's window was on the front of the house, but since Kit's inheritance had shattered the glass, I'd been sleeping upstairs in a room with a window overlooking the backyard. Braun obviously didn't realize I was the one who was still alive, so I assumed he'd been staked out somewhere across the road.

If he didn't come for me in the next two days, I would find him. And I would kill him.

Right before I went to bed, Kit's phone buzzed.

Very well. Saturday afternoon. Your place.

May the best man win.

"I will." I said the words as I typed them. A solemn vow I would uphold.

Chapter 11

The Devil

I followed the tunnel to the barn and grabbed my brush, starting with Ripley as I always did. I leaned my forehead against his. "Today might be the last day I see you."

He lipped my hair in response.

"If it is, I want you to know that I love you, and I didn't mean to leave you."

After letting him outside, I went to Amala's stall and brushed her. "Hey, sweetie." I swallowed the lump that had formed in my throat and plant-ed a kiss between her ears. "I know it's been tough not having Kit around, but soon, I may not be here either." I wrapped my arms around her neck. "I love you, Amala."

I watched Amala trot out to Ripley's side. Even at twenty-three years old, she still seemed spry. Ripley was two years older than her and not nearly as energetic. I hadn't ridden either of them for a couple of years, and I missed it.

I had arranged for Noah to check on them and find them a good home if Braun defeated me. I couldn't bear the thought of them being left to starve.

However, when I defeated Braun, I planned to move to Idaho. I had a ranch near the Sawtooth Mountains that I hadn't visited in over fifty years. There was a chance some people would recognize me, but if it came up, I would say they must be thinking of my mother.

It had been over two hundred years since I'd seen her. No matter how hard I tried I couldn't picture her face or Dad's, but I knew I had his eyes and her hair.

Dwelling on the past wouldn't help me, so I focused on the future. Once I was settled, I would buy new horses to live with Amala and Ripley. Maybe I'd even give riding lessons again.

I followed the tunnel back to the house, hoping to stay out of sight if Braun was watching. I changed out of my barn clothes and into my work-out clothes. A large section of the basement had been turned into a gym for the long winter months when exercising outside was too brutal. I head-ed there, practicing kata until I felt the inevitable pulse of another immortal.

Striding through the tunnel, I breathed deeply, letting each breath go for a count of five. If Braun was about to beat me, it wouldn't be because I wasn't in a good headspace. It would be because he was better than me.

The sky was deep steel blue. Ominous. It promised a snowstorm and made it look like twi-light instead of early afternoon.

I walked around the side of my house to find Braun leaning against his fancy car, staring at the door. I cleared my throat, and he turned toward me. His eyes widened. Then he threw his head back and laughed.

"You." The smile stayed plastered to his face, but it didn't reach his eyes. "So Kit is dead?"

I didn't answer, but I couldn't stop pain from flashing across my face. "Thank you for saving me the trouble of finding you."

He bowed ever so slightly, then waved toward the backyard. "Shall we go somewhere a little more concealed? I'd hate for prying eyes to witness your downfall."

"I'd hate for that, too." I'd learned a long time ago that the Endless men gave me little chance of defeating them in battle, but so far, I was batting 1,000.

Braun stood across from me. His sword dangled loosely from his right hand, the tip nearly touching the ground. "Do you remember me, Keziah?"

Remember him? We'd met before? "No." I searched through my memories but found nothing. "I can't say I do." I took a step closer, and he moved one back. "Even without remembering you, I know enough to want you dead." I cocked my head. "Doesn't say much about the kind of man you are. Does it?"

"Come now, Zie. Think." He grinned. His teeth flashed white against the dark sky.

I'd seen that before.

Two Hundred Years Earlier

I woke up in the forest, gasping for air like a drowning man. My hands flew to my chest expecting to find gaping wounds where the grizzly's claws had torn through my flesh, but there was nothing. No pain. No damage. Nothing except my shredded, blood-soaked clothes to show I'd been mauled.

I lay my head back down and stared straight up. Lodgepole pines surrounded me, stretching toward the sky. Dappled light filtered through their branches. Night would be upon me soon, but I couldn't bring myself to get up just yet. The coppery tang of my blood mixed with the fresh scent of the trees.

The grizzly had been protecting her cubs. I'd startled them, but as far as I could tell, they were long gone.

I stood, dusted myself off the best I could, and pulled my jacket closed over what was left of my blouse.

"A miracle." I tipped my head back and sucked in the air. "Hallejuah!" I staggered forward as unsteady as a newborn foal. "Yes, that has to be it." I was alive and unmarred. I silently thanked God for the miracle He'd given me.

There was no other explanation. No reason I should be alive.

I took another step, letting the belief sink into me. A strange pulsing sensation tore through me. I clutched my head and glanced around, frantically searching the woods for an explanation.

Laughter cut through the trees, and a white smile flashed against their shadows.

The devil himself had come to collect my soul, but I wasn't ready to go. I'd woken to a second chance, and I wasn't about to squander it.

I turned and ran.

Nobody knew these woods better than I did.

I splashed through the creek, exiting where I would leave a trail. After a few paces, I grabbed hold of a low branch, swung my feet off of the ground, and jumped over the stream. I ran on the other side, careful not to be obvious.

I spent the night tucked between the roots of a pine tree and the mountainside. It was uncomfortable, but I saw hide nor hair of the devil.

Present Day

"Ah … there it is. The memory." He tipped his head back and breathed deeply. "You were but a babe, an infant in this immortal life, and somehow you got away." He moved to the side, and I circled with him. "I wanted your heart that day 200 years ago, but now … Well, let's just say it'll be worth the wait."

How could he have found me so quickly back then? Had he truly just stumbled upon me? "Why? Why did you want me dead? You didn't even know me."

"I knew you were destined to be an Endless. Just as I knew Kit would be." He waved his free hand through the air with a flare. "Some of us are destined for greatness—" his lip curled when he looked over at Ripley and Amala grazing "—and some of us to ride horses."

A man who didn't like horses was no friend of mine. "And what makes you so great?"

"Come now, Keziah." He lifted his blade. "It seems you're stalling. If you're afraid to fight me, drop your sword, and I'll end it quickly. No pain just a chance to reunite with Kit if you believe that sort of thing exists for our kind."

I gripped the hilt tighter before realizing that was exactly what he was trying to get me to do. Tension and blind rage would get me nowhere fast. I needed to let my fury go even if just for this battle. "If you wanted to kill me so badly, why'd you send Kit to do it?"

"And get my hands dirty?" He shook his head, making a clicking noise with his tongue. "Where's the fun it that? It was so much better watching him fall in love with you." He fluttered his eyelids and made what I assumed to be kissing noises. "Now, that was one of life's little rewards. You should have seen his desperation. How he tried to talk me into letting you live. That poor boy had it bad." Braun lifted his sword and circled the blade in front of him. "He texted me that you'd been together for twenty years, and he couldn't do it."

Had he? I'd only looked at his unread texts. I hadn't searched through any of the previous ones.

"I told him that if he didn't kill you, I would." The grin that pulled his lips up reminded me of the first time I'd seen him and how I'd believed he was the devil. This man was pure evil. He got pleasure from torment and depravity. "I explained to him all the things I would do to you. It was enough to make him change his mind."

Red coated my gaze, and lava burned through my veins. "You *are* the devil."

He flashed an evil smile and bowed with a flourish. "I wouldn't have allowed him to suffer too long. His usefulness had come to an end."

He took two steps to his right, and I followed. "But how did you best him?"

"Let me show you." I lunged toward him, but he blocked my blow. The clang of our swords echoed through the valley. "I don't know that I want to be the last Endless standing, but I'll be damned if I let it be you."

"You killed your lover, Keziah." He chuckled as he swung. "You're already damned."

Chapter 12

Vengence

Our blades crashed against each other in a steady rhythm. Braun stepped forward, and I glided back, never missing a beat as we moved to the music in a dance I'd been perfecting for the past two hundred years.

Step, strike, block.

Thrust, twirl, lunge.

Dodge, duck, slice.

Our movements were synchronized. The choreography had been ingrained deep inside of me from years of training. For just a moment, I imagined Triston across from me, his blade crashing against mine. His wide smile when he ended the battle, his blue eyes twinkling with pride.

"How did you know Triston?" The words were out of my mouth before I realized I was going to ask him.

His sword struck mine, another note in the song. "Did you think you were the first Endless he trained? The only one?" He glided to the side, and I followed with a strike.

My blade slipped beneath his guard, digging into his side. "First blood."

He danced back, touching the wound. Wincing, he pulled his fingers away, wiping the blood on slacks that cost more than every item in my wardrobe combined. "Enough of this." His free hand slid to his back. My gaze followed the movement, and my lack of attention was repaid with a jab to my thigh.

Sharp pain radiated from the puncture, and blood fell from the wound in a steady flow. I staggered back still watching Braun.

He swung his arm around, holding a 9mm. I dove to the side right before he fired a shot, just barely getting out of the bullet's path.

"Have you no honor?" I wasn't concerned about a bullet going through the Kevlar that protected my heart, but if he shot me in the head, I would be out of commission long enough for him to kill me. No matter what, I couldn't let this bastard walk away.

"This is taking too long, and I have places to be."

Living near the mountains meant boulders littered my yard. Some barely stuck out of the ground, and others were taller than me. I scurried for one of those rocks and reached inside my coat, making sure my gun was still in my holster. Though I would never shoot another endless first, I wasn't opposed to using one in times like this.

I snatched the dagger from my boot and cut the bottom of my shirt off. Slicing through a smaller section, I wadded it up and pressed it against my thigh. Then I wrapped the rest of the fabric strip around my leg. The wound would heal once I stopped exerting myself, but until then, I needed to staunch the bleeding.

"What would Triston say?" I peeked around the stone I was hiding behind.

Braun had sheathed his sword and inched toward me. "Exactly what he said before I shot him."

My heart plummeted to my stomach so quickly that I nearly tumbled over. Triston had been a good, honorable man who hadn't deserved to be betrayed by one of his own.

"Cat got your tongue?" Braun's voice shook me out of my stupor. "The old man had it coming."

The queasy feeling burned beneath my rage. "He had it coming? What the hell is that supposed to mean?" I dashed toward the trees and the Little Laramie River. There wasn't a ton of undergrowth, but there was enough to protect me while I came up with a plan.

Braun rounded the rock I'd been hiding behind and slammed his palm down on it. "Til the last one stands, Keziah. That means when we find an Endless, we kill … no matter what."

"Then why didn't you kill Kit?" I scampered up a cottonwood tree, flattening myself on a thick branch.

He prowled toward my hiding spot, scanning the area with each step. "I planned to, but making him turn on the one he loved … that is where my true enjoyment lies." Stepping into the timber, he put his back to a tree and searched for me. "To gain power is the ultimate goal of an Endless, but to hold power over another is intoxicating."

He moved from tree trunk to tree trunk. Like most people, he didn't bother looking up, but I doubted he'd find me anyway. "Come now, Keziah. You've been a worthy opponent. Don't ruin that by cowering in fear."

I didn't respond, didn't move, and barely breathed. I needed him to wander deeper into the woods for my plan to work.

He crept forward, placing each foot as gingerly as if he were crossing a minefield. "What was it like, Keziah? How did it feel to end Kit's life?" He swung around a tree trunk like he expected to find me on the other side. "Did it turn you on?"

I ground my teeth together and forced myself to stay still. The roaring in my ears drowned out the sounds of nature. I would end this man if it was the last thing I did, but I would not allow him to goad me into attacking before I was ready.

He spun back around, continuing deeper into the trees.

Almost there. He stopped again, and I wondered if he had a sixth sense that kept him out of danger. *Come on.* I forced my clenched jaws apart and tried to calm myself, but the hatred I felt for Braun refused to dissipate.

I pulled my gaze from him and watched a squirrel run up the trunk of a tree near me. It settled on a branch and chittered at me.

Braun looked up at the furry, little snitch, and I could see the realization settle over him. I didn't dare move as he scanned the canopy.

He pointed his gun at the squirrel, and my heart clenched. I was well aware that the bushy-tailed rodents weren't endangered, but this creature didn't deserve to die because I'd hid in a tree. It was innocent and full of life.

Braun sighted the squirrel before lowering his gun. Maybe he liked animals or maybe he realized he should quit making so much noise. No matter what had kept him from pulling the trigger, I was grateful.

The leaves crunched beneath me. *So close. Keep going.* I waited for Braun to walk past my tree. Then as quietly as possible, I dangled from the branch and dropped to the ground behind him. Before he could turn around, I drew my sword and swung.

Chapter 13

Hands Off

*B*raun's gun dropped to the forest floor along with his hand.

He clutched his stump to his chest. "You bitch!" He scrambled back.

"What?" I tipped my head to the side, feigning ignorance. "I thought you lived by our motto. Til the last one stands, right?" This time I stalked toward him. "Or do you only believe in that when you've got the upper hand?" I glanced at the appendage lying on a pile of leaves. "Oh ... too soon for jokes?"

He narrowed his brown eyes at me, and if that look could kill, the inheritance would have ripped my body apart and given my power to Braun. Instead, he turned and fled.

I pulled my dagger from my boot and threw it. It sailed through the air, flipping end over end before striking Braun in the back of the neck.

When he fell to the ground, I knew my blade had struck true, severing his brain stem.

If he was a normal human, he'd be dead, but he was an Endless, and if I waited too long his hand would grow back, and he would suck in another breath. I strode toward him, knelt beside his body, and jerked my blade free. Then I rolled him over, unbuttoned his shirt, and removed his Kevlar vest.

I held my dagger over his chest. It didn't seem right to kill an unarmed, unconscious man, but he was the reason Kit was dead. He'd killed Triston. I hesitated only a moment before plunging the blade into his heart.

His body arched, and he sucked in a gasping breath, staring up at me with bulging eyes.

"Til the last one stands." I backed away from him. Unlike with Kit, I didn't care if he felt alone when he died.

Golden light spilled from Braun's chest. It crept over his body like fog rolling in and spread across the ground. Tendrils branched off, stretching for me.

The shimmering energy spun up into the air, the largest cyclone I'd ever seen. *How old had Braun been?*

The vortex broke the smaller branches from the trees as it gained speed. The squirrel quit yelling and zipped off, hopping from limb to limb as it rushed away from the chaos surrounding me.

Coils of power wrapped around my arms and legs, lifting me off the ground. I hovered above Braun's body, glowing brighter than a supernova. The force crashed into me, a tsunami of energy coursing through my body, drowning me beneath its strength.

I screamed, freeing all of the hatred and rage that I'd held onto since Kit's death.

Braun's power slammed into me, striking me like a thunderbolt. It merged with mine, slithering through my body.

Slimy. Greasy.

I shivered with disgust, loathing that any part of him survived and that it would live inside of me even more.

The last of the light struck me. My skin glowed, growing brighter until I convulsed, and the maelstrom of power exploded out of me, felling trees and dropping me on the ground where Braun's body was nothing more than a pile of glimmering dust.

Chapter 14

Shared Grief

Dusk had fallen by the time I staggered back to my house. My body still ached from the inheritance rebuilding my muscles to accommodate Braun's power. I ran a hot bath, stripped off my clothes, and eased myself into the tub, soaking until the water turned too cold to linger any longer.

I'd thought that ending Braun would feel better. Different.

But Kit was still gone.

I was still alone.

I pulled on my comfy pajamas, went to the kitchen, and made myself a cup of hot chocolate.

After starting a fire, I sat on the couch and grabbed *Initiate* by Jenny Sandiford off the coffee table. I'd been slowly working my way through the novel when I needed something to take my mind off of Kit and Braun and living forever.

I sat at a picnic table in Labonte Park, waiting for Noah to show up. I had no desire to relive Kit's death, but I'd made a promise, and I would keep it. He parked his Equinox along the curb and strode toward me with his hands tucked into his coat pockets. A stocking cap covered his blond hair, keeping it from blowing into his eyes.

"You have no idea how relieved I was to get your call." He sat across from me and put his phone on the table. "How are you doing?"

I stared over his shoulder into the distance, not seeing anything, and lifted my shoulder. "I'd like to get this over with so I can move on."

"Yeah, I can understand that." He fidgeted with his phone. "Do you mind if I record you? It's easier than writing everything down."

"Sure." I waved at his phone. "Whatever you need."

Thirteen Days Ago

Kit walked out of the bathroom, tucking his bronze dress shirt into his black slacks. He sat on the end of the bed and pulled on his dressy cowboy boots.

Twenty years. How had I gotten so lucky to land him? I slid on my little, black dress. "Zip me?" I turned my back to him, looking over my shoulder.

He leaned close. His warm breath caressed my neck. His fingers brushed against my skin, leaving a trail of goosebumps in their wake, as he slowly tugged the zipper up. He settled his hands on my waist, holding me in front of the mirror. "You look amazing, Ziah." His pupils were dilated, and his gaze kept dropping to my lips.

He spun me around and traced his finger in a path from my ear to my shoulder. "I can't wait to take this dress off of you later." He leaned in, gently brushing his lips over mine. Before he could pull away, I deepened the kiss.

When his tongue slid over mine, I considered not bothering with going to dinner. I pulled away. "We better go now." I wiped my lipstick off his mouth. "Or I won't want to."

"And that would be bad?" He laughed and grabbed my hand. "I don't care what I do as long as I'm with you."

Present Day

"I saw the two of you go into Old Corral." Noah fiddled with his sleeve. "I ended up sitting near you that night."

I traced my finger along the top of the mesh metal picnic table. "We were going to go to Altitude in Laramie, but eating in Centennial meant we had more time …" Talking about sex with somebody I wasn't involved with was new to me, and I felt my cheeks heating up at the thought of sharing that with him. "… to ourselves."

Thirteen Days Ago

Kit pressed his hand against my back and led me outside to his truck. Millions of stars dotted the sky. "It's a beautiful night." He reached around me to open my door.

I stopped him, wrapping my arms around his waist and pulling him closer to me. "It's a perfect night." I held his gaze for several seconds before cupping his cheeks in my hands. "I love you, Kit. Today. Tomorrow. Always." I drew his mouth down to mine, touching my lips to his, teasing him.

He growled and tugged me closer.

Tingles started in my chest and spread lower.

His mouth hovered above mine for a moment before crashing down. His tongue parted my lips and delved deeper.

A low moan escaped me, and I twined my leg around his. His hand slid down my back to my butt.

The Old Corral's door opened, and a beam of light shone on my face.

"Let's take this home, Ziah." Kit opened the truck's door and waited for me to climb inside before shutting it.

When he finally walked around to his side, he was looking down at his phone. He hopped inside, and the light and passion that had been on his face moments before was gone, replaced by a blank mask.

"What's wrong?" I reached for his hand, but he started the truck and put it in reverse, backing out and pulling onto the road.

He shook his head. "Nothing." He slid his fingers through mine. "Let's get home and pick up where we left off."

Present Day

"I saw you in the parking lot." Noah's cheeks reddened. "You both seemed ... eager. I thought it would be an uneventful evening for me."

Heat clawed up my neck. I cleared my throat, reached into my pocket, and pulled out Kit's phone. "I'm keeping this, but you can take pictures of the texts if you want." I opened up the message app and clicked on Braun's name. Then I scrolled back to September 17th.

Why isn't she dead yet?

I can't do it. I love her.

If you don't do it, I will make her suffer while you watch. Do you want to relive Natalia's death?

You could've saved her so much pain by ending her yourself.

Why are you doing this?

I gave you your life. In return, you agreed to do everything I asked of you.

Please.

Don't make me do this.

I could have put a bullet through both of your heads while you were zipping her dress up tonight. You didn't even know I was watching.

I'm begging you, Braun. Please.

Please let me keep her.

Do it, or I will.

We've been together 20 years. I can't kill her. Think of Natalia.

Do you remember what she looked like when I finished with her?

Please.

I'll be expecting your confirmation tomorrow.
Don't let me down.

Noah looked up from Kit's phone. His eyebrows were pinched together. "Why didn't you sense him?"

"My best guess." I dragged my hands down my face. "Sniper rifle. I'm not sure why he didn't use that when he came for Kit Saturday. He must've thought he could beat him without it."

He shook his head. "I'm glad you killed him. What would it mean for the world if someone so dishonorable was the last?"

"Nothing good." I watched a squadron of pelicans land on Stink Lake. "Do you know who Natalia was? What happened to her?"

His green eyes glistened. "Yeah." His voice was hoarse. "Well, not really, but we heard her screams for days." He swallowed hard. "It's all in my book."

"Do you mind if I keep it?"

He waved at the binder that sat on the bench next to me. "No, go ahead. I can always send you a copy once it's published, too."

"I won't be here." I rubbed my chest. Moving away meant saying goodbye, and even though I needed to, I wasn't ready to let go of Kit. Unfortunately, I'd stayed in this area too long already.

He stretched his hand across the table, settling it on top of mine. "Your Chronicler will let me know where you end up."

"Of course." There I was sitting across from one, and yet I'd forgotten that someone was watching my every move.

I steeled myself before telling Noah about waking up to find Kit kneeling above me in bed. Remembering Kit's betrayal left me numb. With every word, my chest tightened further and further, and I wondered if it would ever loosen.

Tears silently trailed down Noah's cheeks. His green irises brightened as the whites of his eyes reddened. His hand tightened over mine, and I didn't feel quite so alone, knowing that someone else shared my grief.

Chapter 15

Moving On

"What will you do now?" I grabbed the binder, and the two of us strolled to our vehicles.

He fiddled with the strap of his bag. "I'll finish writing Kit's story. Then I'll be assigned to a new Endless."

"So, you go wherever, whenever they tell you to?" I couldn't imagine having somebody control my life like that. The twenty-five years I'd spent in Centennial was the longest I'd ever stayed anywhere. Being able to go where I wanted and do what I wanted were things I didn't think I'd ever want to give up.

Freedom was something that should never be taken for granted.

"For now." His gaze drifted to mine and then away again as if something was making him uncomfortable.

I grabbed his arm just above the elbow. "What is it? Something's making you nervous."

"Well ... your Chronicler wants to retire." He bit his bottom lip, pulling it into his mouth. "How would you feel about me requesting you as an assignment?"

I flipped my hands palms up and shrugged. "You do you. If you want to follow me around, that's your choice, but I'm moving back to my ranch near Hailey, Idaho." I watched his face, wondering how he'd react, but he didn't give me any clue as to how he felt about it. He would definitely make a better card player than me. "I'm hoping to be out of here by the end of the week or early next week at the latest."

"Idaho. Huh." He patted his bag. "It'll be a month or more before I would take over. I've got a book to finish."

I packed everything I was taking with me and hired a nice couple to watch the house. Then I loaded Amala and Ripley into the trailer and drove to my home outside of Hailey. The nine-hour drive turned into a little over twelve hours by the time I stopped to check on my horses.

When I finally pulled into my driveway, the sun was just about to dive below the horizon. My headlights shone on the log cabin that I hadn't called home in over fifty years. After defeating Braun, I'd called Jami and Jesse, the twenty-something-year-old sister and brother who took care of this house, to let them know I'd be returning. The front porch looked warm and welcoming, but before I could step inside, I needed to tend to my horses.

I hopped out of the truck and stretched before opening the trailer and grabbing Ripley's reins. I petted his side as I led him to his stall in the barn. Then I went back for Amala. She nuzzled my shoulder as I led her into her new home.

Clean hay lined the stalls, and grain and fresh water waited for my horses. Despite their accommodations, they pawed at the ground and looked around nervously.

"Hey, guys, I know this is a big change for you." I kept my voice low, hoping to soothe them. "It's a big change for me, too, but we're going to get through this." I patted each of them, then walked to the barn door, holding it open. "I'll come back out in the morning and show you around your new home."

I dragged myself to my truck, pulled my duffle out, and staggered to the front door. It had been a long day of driving, and I was beat. I pulled my boots off, trudged up the steps, dropped my bag next to the door, and fell onto the bed. I was asleep before I had a chance to think about it.

Chapter 16

New Life

A month after moving back to Idaho I had four new horses, and riding lessons were in full swing.

I folded my arms over the top of the fence, planted a foot on the bottom railing, and watched Jami and Jesse race through the indoor arena. Seeing them on Phantom, the all-white mare, and Eclipse, the black stallion, filled me with a peace that I hadn't felt since before Kit tried to kill me. The cadence of the horses' hooves and the laughter of the riders soothed my soul.

They slowed to a trot and walked the horses around the arena before stopping across the fence from me.

"All right!" Jesse jumped off Eclipse's back and flipped his long, golden-brown hair behind him. "Who won?" Before anyone had a chance to answer, he pointed his thumbs at his chest. "Me. That's who."

Jami rolled her green eyes and dismounted. Her caramel-colored braid swung in front of Phantom, and the mare lipped at it. "In your dreams, rat."

Their good-natured ribbing continued while I climbed the fence. "You two look like you could be twins."

"We are." A shit-eating grin tugged Jesse's lips up. "The Wonder Twins." He held his hands in front of his face with his palms facing out, then moved them in a circular motion.

Jami nodded. "Yep. People wonder why we're not twins, but it's because I'm two years older than the rat."

I couldn't remember a time when I'd been as carefree as these two. When I was younger than Jami, I'd been married off to Cyrus, a man I didn't love and who was incapable of loving me. Instead of training his horses, I'd been stuck inside doing the cooking and cleaning.

So much had changed in my lifetime. Some of those changes were good. Indoor plumbing for example. Some weren't.

"Wonder twins, huh?" I jumped down between the horses. Phantom skittered back a step, but Eclipse nuzzled me. I petted his neck. "It seems fitting for the two of you. Take the horses back to the barn, brush them, then come up to the house."

Leaving them to their duties, I walked the path to the back door. Fat, lazy flakes drifted down from the sky. They clung to my eyelashes and piled on the ground.

A pulse slammed into me. Wild and erratic.

A new Endless.

After all this time, the chaotic feeling still brought back memories of my rebirth, making my heart race and dread settle in my stomach. The desire to flee made me feel like a timid hare. I sucked in a calming breath and remembered that I had been a predator far longer than I had ever been prey.

I turned and scanned the area. Ponderosa pines surrounded my property, hiding my house from the road.

Someone stumbled out of the trees. His hands were pressed to his skull. His clothes were covered in blood. "What is … happening … to me?" He continued staggering toward me. "I should be dead. I know I died." He stopped and stared at me. His eyes wide. "Am I a ghost? Did my spirit not move on?"

I looked over my shoulder. Jami and Jesse should be with the horses for some time still. Stepping toward the man, I held my hands up and calmed my voice. "Come inside with me, and I'll explain everything." I walked to the back door and held it open for him, waiting for him to decide if he wanted to trust me or not.

"You're—" He bent forward, clutching his head. "You're like me. Aren't you?"

My gaze darted to the barn again, hoping we were far enough away that we wouldn't be overheard. "Come inside. You can get cleaned up, and I'll tell you about your new life."

"New life!" He dropped his hands to his sides and fisted them. "I don't want a new life. I like the life I have. I have a good job, a fiancée, and a cat. I'm good."

I waved my hand to the door. "Come inside …" I hesitated long enough that he realized I was asking his name.

"Dusty." He stepped past me, looking over his shoulder as he went inside. "And you are?"

"Ziah." I led him through the sunroom, dining room, and living room to the stairs. "I'll see if I can find some clothes that will fit you. You can grab a shower. Then we'll talk." I walked up the steps behind him, ready in case he toppled over.

When we got to the top, I had him wait in the hall while I dug through Jesse's dresser, hoping he had something Dusty could wear. I settled on a pair of sweatpants and a t-shirt. As wiry as Jesse was, I hoped they would fit the stockier man. After handing the clothes off to him and setting out some clean towels, I walked downstairs and waited on the back deck. Snow dusted me, but I didn't feel its chill.

Jami and Jesse ran down the path, throwing snowballs at each other. As soon as they saw me, they folded their hands behind their backs and walked the rest of the way. When they stood in front of me, I handed them some cash. "Would you two mind running into Hailey to pick up the pizza? I called in an order to 2 Talls Pizzeria."

"Pee-zah!" Jesse's voice dropped a few octaves. Then he grabbed the money and bounded back down the path.

"You might have to wait." I flipped my hand up. When I ordered the pizza, I told them to add some extra time. I needed the siblings gone while I talked to Dusty. They didn't know about the Endless, and I hoped to keep it that way. "There's some extra in there if you two want to get a soda or something while you wait."

"Thanks." Jami grinned at me, then took off after her brother. "I'm driving."

I walked inside and leaned against the sunroom's door. Dusty's arrival complicated things, but I couldn't turn him away. Triston had taught me better than that.

I grabbed a pitcher, filled it with ice water, and set it on the table along with two glasses. Then I paced. I stopped in front of the fireplace. The wood was stacked, and the flue was clean, so I grabbed the matches off the mantel and lit the kindling.

Then I sat at the table, drumming my fingers on its wooden surface while I waited for Dusty to emerge. I knew how this part played out. He would stand in front of the mirror and touch the places his wounds had been. The whole while wondering if he'd gone mad. I just hoped he didn't take too long.

After several minutes, I couldn't take it anymore. I ran up the stairs and knocked on the bathroom door. "I know patience is a virtue, but it isn't one of mine." I leaned against the wall. "We need to talk before my hired hands come back."

He opened the door wearing only the sweatpants. Water dripped from the tips of his short brown hair down his pecs. He looked at me, his blue eyes wide, and then at himself. "How ... how am I alive?" He gingerly tapped his chest. "There was a chunk of metal sticking out of me."

"Come sit at the table." I walked down the stairs. "Do you want something to drink?"

He followed me, each footfall a loud, defeated thump. "I just wanna know what the hell is going on."

"We are Endless." I stepped into the dining room, pulled out his chair, and waited for him to sit before taking the seat across from him. The golden wood walls were the cheeriest in the house. A dusty rose, cream, and tan rug sat beneath the table, and horse pictures were hung around the room. "That feeling—"

"That was awful. I thought my head was going to explode."

I remembered the first time I'd felt another Endless, and a shiver traveled down my spine. "You'll get used to it eventually, but yeah, it sucks.

You're going to feel it every time another of us is around."

He planted his elbows on the table and held his face in his hands. His desperation was so familiar to me. Not only had I been there and felt it, I'd seen it so many times over the years. "So, what do you mean by endless?"

"The Endless are a group of immortals."

He snorted but, at my glare, waved me on.

"I look like I'm thirty-three years old, but I'm actually two hundred thirty-three." I held his gaze as I spoke, hoping he would believe me, but knowing he most likely wouldn't. "I was killed by a grizzly in 1824." I'd rehashed this story so many times that it no longer fazed me. The first few times I'd talked about it, my heart had raced, and I'd glanced over my shoulder expecting to see the mother bear behind me. "We will never get older, and the only way either of us can die is if our hearts are irreparably damaged."

He gazed down at his chest for a moment but then looked back at me. His mouth slackened, and he slumped in his chair while absentmindedly rubbing the spot where he'd been impaled. "I thought you were going to tell me what's going on, not feed me some bullshit story." He slammed his chair back and jumped to his feet.

I walked into the kitchen and grabbed a knife from the block on the cabinet. Then I sauntered back to the dining room, holding his gaze.

"What are you doing?" He backed away from me, and his eyes widened.

I had more experience with horses than with people, but even I could read his reaction. I held my hands up, hoping to calm him. "Just watch, okay?" I dragged the blade from my elbow to my wrist. Sharp, throbbing pain followed the knife's path as I cut clear through to the bone.

"What the hell?" His gaze flicked from my arm to my eyes and back again.

Gold energy danced over the wound, sparking as the muscles knitted themselves back together. The relief was instantaneous, a cooling balm that numbed any pain. The healing process was amazing to watch. Beautiful in all honesty. The shimmering ribbons of energy reminded me of the golden bows wrapped around Christmas presents or the garland draped around the trees. It undulated and danced, twirling and whirling until not even a slight blemish marred the skin.

"If you cut yourself, the same would happen." I strode to the kitchen, dropped the knife in the sink, and leaned my hip against the countertop.

He plopped back down in his chair. "Okay … let me get this straight." He pointed at me and then at himself. "You're telling me that we're going to live forever."

I tucked my hands in my pockets, hoping to relax him further. "Something like that."

"Something like that?" He tipped his head to the side.

The next part wasn't so easy, but he needed to know what his life had become. No matter how I said it, some of the new Endless decided to battle the second they learned about the game. Some, unable to handle the idea of killing, ended themselves. Some threw up, spewing the last meal of their first life. And some took it in stride. "You won't die of old age or disease, but you can be killed."

He perked up, and a slow smile tugged at his mouth. He bit his lip, trying to stop it, but it built until it covered his entire face. Without the fear and shock, he looked younger than I first thought. Maybe upper twenties, not the mid-thirties like I initially believed. "So what is the price of this immortality?"

Chapter 17

It's All Fun and Games

$\mathcal{I}$ pictured Kit hovering above me. Moonlight glinted off his blade. I shook my head. That was the worst that could happen, but my second life had been filled with so much good. It had freed me from Cyrus' wrath. Back then, a woman who couldn't conceive children was more worthless than a runt pig. Even though it had been a loveless marriage, I had hated myself for not being able to make him a father.

My first death freed me, granting me the ability to defy the conventions set for women and to live my own life. Triston had taken me in, shown me how to survive, and taught me how to pan for gold, and that money had lasted for all my subsequent lives, allowing me to do what I loved: raise horses and give riding lessons.

And the last twenty years …

Warmth flooded through me when I remembered the first time I'd seen Kit smile at me. Dimples.

A soft chuckle escaped me. For the first time since I'd woken up that night, I thought of Kit without hurt and betrayal piercing my heart.

Ripley's and Amala's nickers filled my mind. They were to be the start of a new herd, but when Kit entered my life, I'd taken time to myself, had fun, and truly lived life.

I pictured Jami and Jesse racing across the arena. Their laughter and playful teasing brought the joy of youth back into my life.

"I'm not going to lie. The cost is high." I leaned forward, folding my arms on the table as I did. "You have to leave your family and friends behind."

"What?" His mouth hung open, and he stared at me through hard, blue eyes. "I'm getting married next weekend!"

"I'm sorry." My chest tightened, and my heart felt too heavy to fit inside it. "Mortals aren't to know about us."

He jumped from his seat and paced. "I get in one stupid car wreck, and my life's over?"

"No." I huffed. "That's what happens to most people. You got in one stupid car wreck, and you have a second chance at life. Your slate's been wiped clean."

His body was rigid, and the muscles in his arms were defined. His intense glare didn't stop me from continuing.

"Your mistakes are gone. Any idiotic thing you did in your youth is erased. Your life as you know it is over, but it would've been either way. Most people who die stay dead." I strode toward him and shoved my finger at his chest. "You were given a second chance at life. Don't blow it."

He crumpled forward, resting his head on the table. His shoulders shook. "What is Maggie … going t-to do?"

"She'll grieve." My heart ached for this woman I didn't even know. "It'll take time, but eventually, she'll move on."

He peered up at me. "You make it sound so easy."

I huffed out a laugh that lacked all humor. "It's not easy at all." I walked to the cabinet and pulled out a lowball glass. I grabbed a bottle of whiskey off the top of the fridge. "I need a drink. You?"

"Make it a double." As soon as I handed his drink to him, he threw it back and set his glass on the table. "Who'd you lose?"

I slammed my shot, then ran my finger around the rim. "My boyfriend of twenty years. Only a couple of months ago."

The sympathy that softened his eyes was nearly unbearable to look at. I poured another drink, then held the bottle up. He nodded. "There's more to immortality."

"Of course, there is." He knocked back his whiskey. "Lay it on me."

"Our life is a game." I used air quotes around the word game. "Til the last one stands."

Leaning back, he folded his arms over his chest. "What in God's name is that supposed to mean?"

"It means you're lucky that you stumbled onto my property. Not all Endless believe in training those new to the game." I thought of Braun and how he told me I'd escaped him. "It means you should stay here. I have a room in the basement you can use. It means we should start training as soon as possible." I drummed my fingers on the tabletop, careful not to leave fingernail marks in the epoxy. I glanced at the clock. "Jami and Jesse should be returning any moment with pizza. You are more than welcome to join us, but if you tell them what we are, I will end you."

Chapter 18

Training

My sword crashed against Dusty's, forcing his to the ground. "You're getting better."

"Sure." He picked his practice blade up and strode over to the bench. He grabbed a towel and wiped it over his head, making his brown hair spiky. His locks had grown since showing up here. The added length looked better on him.

While Jami and Jesse were doing chores and taking online college courses, Dusty and I devoted eight hours a day to training in the gym in the basement. The floor was covered with black mats, and weapons hung on the walls. I preferred spend-

"Sorry to intrude." He thrust a package toward me. "I wanted you to have Kit's book."

I inched my hand forward, and goosebumps pebbled my arm. A strange combination of emotions welled inside of me. Gratefulness and resentment. They twisted together until I thought I might throw up. "Thanks." I looked over my shoulder, knowing I wouldn't see anyone there. Dusty had gone to the barn with Jami and Jesse for a temporary break from training this morning. I'd been about to get him when I noticed Noah. "Do you want to come in?"

"Please." He shoved his hands into his pockets. "I have something I'd like to talk to you about."

I held the book up, pinched my lips together, and lifted one side of my mouth in an unspoken question.

"No." He shook his head and stared at his feet. "Something else." His voice quieted until I could barely hear him. "Something I shouldn't." He stepped inside and pulled his snow-covered winter boots off.

The sun shone through the two-story tall windows that surrounded the fireplace, so I didn't bother flipping the lights on. I set Kit's book on the coffee table, then perched on the edge of my tan recliner, hoping he'd realize I didn't have a lot of time to spare. Dusty's training couldn't wait too long.

Noah settled on the couch with his elbows on his knees and his face hidden by his hands. "This goes against everything I promised when I became a Chronicler."

I waited for him to continue, hoping my silence would prod him on.

"Bill Turner has been seen around the Sawtooth Mountains." He slitted his fingers and peeked through them.

I'd heard the name before, but except for *Pirates of the Caribbean*, I couldn't remember where or when. "I assume you don't mean Bootstraps Bill." A slight smile edged one side of his mouth up. "So I'm drawing a blank here."

"No." All traces of humor left his expression. "This Bill is ruthless. He sensed an Endless approaching and shot his wife, Wendy, in the leg so he could get away." He popped up and started pacing. "They were married nearly thirty years." He reached the fireplace and spun to face me. Raising his hands, he smacked them against the air in time with his words. "Thirty years, and he just left her to die."

I couldn't believe how shocked he sounded. He'd just written Kit's life story. He knew Kit had tried to kill me, not just leave me wounded. "So ... what I'm hearing is that a lot of immortals are bastards."

He stopped moving and stared at me. "Oh." His eyes widened, and his hand flew to his mouth when he realized what he'd said. "Oh. Ziah, I wasn't thinking."

"I gathered that." I gestured toward the couch, hoping he'd sit again. "What does this have to do with me?"

His gaze darted around the room before settling on me. He leaned forward and lowered his voice to a whisper. "It's rumored he can sense new Endless, and we believe he's hunting Dusty."

"I thought you didn't take sides." I slumped back in my chair, making it rock. I shouldn't have taken it personally. He'd been Kit's Chronicler, not mine, but I couldn't help but think that if he'd told me about Braun, everything would be different.

Noah lowered his head. "We're not supposed to." He met my gaze, and I saw the grief written on his face. "I can't let it happen again. Evil can't keep winning because we stand aside and allow it to thrive."

It seemed I wasn't the only one who felt guilty about Kit's death. I sucked in a breath and let go of some of my anger. "Thank you for letting me know." I glanced at Kit's story. "You didn't come all the way out here just to bring me that, did you?"

His Adam's apple bounced in his throat before he shook his head. "No, your Chronicler retired." His eyes darted away from mine. "I know I could've saved both of you if I'd spoken up, and I will regret that for the rest of my life, but if you're still okay with it, I'd like to be your Chronicler."

"Like I said before, you do you."

He sagged in relief. "Thank you, Ziah. I wasn't sure the powers that be were going to let me take over, but they decided the knowledge I already have of you is irreplaceable." He walked to the door and slipped one boot on.

I followed him, leaning against the banister at the bottom of the stairs. "While I appreciate the information, don't get yourself in trouble for me."

He finished pulling his boots on and lacing them up. When he stood, his green eyes were solemn. "I don't think either of us is ready to lose another good Endless."

"Whether he likes it or not, Dusty is part of my family now." After vowing not to get close to anyone again, I was surprised to find out I meant it. "And come hell or high water, I'll protect him."

**The best way to help an author
or to thank them for writing
a book that captivated you
is to leave a review.**

If you enjoyed this book or even if you didn't,
please go online and leave a review.

Reviews sell books.

Without them, authors struggle to gain traction.

Be sure to pick up every novel in the series
to fully enjoy the experience, and follow these
authors as they explore your favorite characters.

Mandi Oyster
Molly Chase
Ren Blake
Samantha Shaye
Sophea Chan
T. S. Devon

Acknowledgments

Holy cow! Can you believe this is book #10?

As always, I want to thank my hubby first. Jeff lets me bounce ideas off of him, and even though I don't incorporate all of them, they help me find my way. And besides that, he's an all around amazing man. I would be lost without him.

My kids for supporting and encouraging me and wanting more.

My parents for giving me a deep appreciation of nature and reading, for giving me the courage to follow my dreams, and always being there. I miss you every day, Mom, but I know you're watching over me.

Next up, Jenny Sandiford, author extraordinaire, thank you for reading this and encouraging me and for just being amazing!

Thank you, T.S. Devon, for asking me to be a part of this. I had so much fun writing this novella, and it never would have been on my radar if not for you.

And, of course, you the reader. Thank you so much for picking up my book and reading it. You are amazing!

Thank You!

If you liked this story, you can join my mailing
list.

Drop by my website <u>MandiOyster.com</u>,
or if you have any comments,
shoot me a note at mandi@mandioyster.com.

I am always happy to hear from people who've
read my work. I try to answer every email I
receive.

Facebook – <u>https://www.facebook.com/</u>
<u>MandiOysterAuthor</u>
Instagram – <u>https://www.instagram.com/</u>
<u>mandioyster/</u>
My web page – MandiOyster.com

About the Author

Mandi Oyster lives in Southwest Iowa in the middle of an enchanted forest where unicorns, fairies, and dragons abound. At least, that's what she assumes when she looks out into the trees. Her husband, two kids (when they're not away at college), four cats, and two chinchillas share the house with her.

Besides being an author, she also runs her own editing business and works full-time as a digital prepress supervisor for a local printshop.

You can find her online at:
https://www.MandiOyster.com
https://www.facebook.com/MandiOysterAuthor
https://instagram.com/MandiOyster/